LOVE CONCOCTION

The Realization of What Love Is

by Moses Rondel

Contents

CHAPTER

AGE 17

WHY IS THERE EVEN SUCH a thing as different genders, male and female? Instead of just having no gender? Obviously it is largely for reproduction. What biological processes sparks the gender differentiation in a human being at the fetal development stage? Is it really just the X and Y chromosomal programming of the incoming spermatozoa?

No! The amniotic fluid in the growing human fetus contains a certain amount of testosterone that is not present in female fetuses. Could this testosterone be the spark that makes baby boys? And how about the sexual physical and mental changes that occur during puberty that further differentiates the different sexes.

Once again, testosterone is the primary hormone present in a teenage male's body as they go through puberty. And estrogen/estradiol for females. So the answer is totally, completely and undeniably hormones. No need for dating books or dating advice, etc. Within all humans exists the capacity to attract each other and then to mate. It all depends on the hormones. Hormones lead to feelings > leading to actions.

Hallelujah!

CHAPTER

AGE 17

COULD YOU BE THE GIRL

Could you be the girl?
Could you be the one?
Who finally makes me whole
Becomes the mate of my soul

Are you able to know?
How I feel in my heart?
The feeling is real and true
The feeling is all I do

Am I compelled to know you?
To see you, and be near you?
Is it my destiny to fall for,
And be yours, at thy door?

CHAPTER

AGE 18

SUPER QUICK ONE RIGHT NOW. What do women want? Throughout so many years of my life I have been totally lost. Specifically, all throughout the years of puberty. It's probably not due so much to the phytoestrogens exposure back then, since I wasn't exposed to all that much of it (only some processed foods I ate probably had it). But I have never truly understood what it is women wanted.

Also, throughout my teens, I had come to the conclusion that they desired guys with money and wealth and good jobs and power and status, etc. But even then, this picture is not wholly accurate. My international experiences mainly led me to this conclusion. I also drew inspiration from evolutionary theory of survival of the strongest. And stuff David DeAngelo preached.

But really, this epiphany has given me the answer. This love concoction I have been taking. Women want the same things natural men want to offer them. They want a quality relationship with someone who is fun to spend time with and who complements them. Someone who can take care of and complement them (compatibility wise). Someone who is fun to talk to and spend time with. Going out on romantic or otherwise exciting dates with.

Yes. Guys with a lot of money and power can provide these better, but by no means is this assured or absolutely needed. A minimum standard expected of the guy is probably a regular income and a place of their own (no living at home with parents!). But I emphasize it is the great love feeling she gets when she spends time with, and chats with the guy which she really responds to.

Renting is acceptable although she would prefer a guy who owns the house. So yes, women definitely go for a guy with means (if you girls want guys who own houses then yes, this is a slight gold digger mentality - don't deny that many women are a tiny bit of a gold digger - but this is OK... it's all in the evolutionary programming). Women need to put so much effort into raising kids, the least a guy can do is go out into the world and make money! He has his entire 20's to achieve this. DARE YOU SAY I DON'T KNOW WHAT I AM SAYING ?

Women want guys who care for them and who

show love. They can give you drama because they can be moody, but if the guy cares enough for her he will still be there (within reasonable limits). He will prioritize her. It's all down to the feeling the guys should feel for her. The feeling tells me everything. Not dreams. Not logical analysis. Today, the feeling has told me what it is women want out of a partner.

Yes. Women want men who want them back! They want the things a man, a natural man wants to give her to make her happy. Happy wife, happy life right?

Why or how do I know this? Because I really want to flirt with girls now (flirting is fun). I don't feel so bad again if the girl rejects me, or deviates away from me, or shows uncertainty (this is different to a lack of interest – a lack of interest is generally bad, but if she is merely uncertain about you then this is OK). Yes. This is the dating game. I want to kiss girls. I want to go out and spend time with them watching movies at a cinema, and eating dinner, or drinking coffee or drinks at a cafe. And of course I would like to make love to the right girl.

She wants a guy who shows he is really interested in her by (him) pursuing the relationship a bit. And as a guy, I (more) like to take part in this mating dance now (within limits). It's been a while but I am starting to remember.

Of course a guy who is absolutely stunning to her (if he's super attractive, or famous, or successful, etc.) she will generally not require him to work too hard. And she will show constant interest and availability. But she still wants to see that he loves her. The way this love is communicated may very well be in gifts or time spent or whatever. It is different somewhat for different girls but the general trend is the same (for all or most typical girls). This is quality time spent together. And money or means contributed.

What else do I want now in a girl. I want a decent (non courtesan/non slutty) physically attractive girl I can date and talk with. Someone who shows a strong interest in me back. Someone who I want to kiss in the lips and show off in public (her being pretty will help a lot in this regard, but hair design, makeup and clothing, and personal grooming can go a long way here towards this objective). I don't like girls who are too short. Or girls who are too skinny or fat.

So deducing all this, I think I have figured out now what women want. I read a brief book description from an author once where he said; women demand love and men demand respect. So true. Women need to never be disrespectful of a man's work or decisions. This could kill a relationship.

Women therefore also want a man whose job she at least somewhat likes or admires. If she likes his job, this also means she will respect it. If she doesn't like garbage collectors for example, then she would probably never give him a chance in the first place. And this is probably a good thing cos that garbage collector will demand she respect his work.

I am starting to know! Now I just need to prove it with actions. To pick up. To flirt. To go on great dates. And to be intimate and make love.

Women want someone who is easy and natural to talk with. Someone respectful in society. Conclusion again: women want things in a man, which the man himself wants to give her. Whether this means the man needs to chase her more, or work harder in the relationship, or in his job (to earn money, power, status, etc.), it's all the same.

And women naturally also want to be the person that men naturally like. Someone who is well groomed. Pleasant to the eye. Feminine and caring of children. Sexy (not overweight). And yes girls, I am saying it is OK for you to want to go shopping with a guy and have him pay for items. Because natural men want to give you this to make you happy (which will make him happy - even before you give him 'base intimacy', although the intimacy is the jackpot reward). The problem is only if you take what he buys for you or gives you (e.g. he might drive you to work everyday) and then not show your happiness or appreciation. If you show the appreciation, he will become happy and that is money well spent. After all, he worked hard for that money.

This is all natures way. A guy who is of normal hormones will love the opportunity to pay things for a girl. Only estradiol inclined or phytoestrogen guys (like those dudes in the gold digger YouTube videos driving nice cars) would not understand.

If I go out with a girl, I crave the opportunity to pay for her. It's an opportunity not to be missed. Paying is not a burden!

I SEE THE LIGHT PEOPLE ! DO YOU ?

CHAPTER

AGE 18

POEM FOR THIS TIK TOK FEMALE

Speechless
Dazzling
Adorable
Sensatiable

A breathless wonder
Of seething beauty
Blessing the Earth
With her gorgeous worth

Her god given femininity
And mesmerizing walk
Brings love at first sight
And pleasure upon light

The face of a white angel
Flickering hair of boyhood dreams
Palm pressed against the chest
This is tik tok footage at its best

My vow today, which I proudly display
Is that I will find you near, when my time is here
I will scour every stone, to find you alone
In this god given Earth, where
we've all been birth'd

I will seek till then, your wonderful soul
As seen in, your enchanting glow
So that on the day where we finally do meet
It will be the absolute best,
most memorable greet.

CHAPTER

AGE 18

DAMN. JUST FINISHED WATCHING MANY parts of Star Trek Voyager S1 Ep 14. A very, very interesting episode. It's about the character B'elana Torres being turned temporarily into human form. Basically it is the first (and to my knowledge only) episode, where she is acting as herself without any of the costume makeup of her alien Klingon character.

But basically I just thought she was such an attractive woman. The transformation was incredible. It's because I have watched so many episodes (practically all others) where she is a major character in it, and her usual Klingon form is just so unattractive. Not just in her appearance but also her personality. Her Klingon character is so aggressive and loud and unattractive.

And even during the occasional time where her character is acting or behaving in a gentle way, she is still not attractive. Her looks just makes you ignore her. She is just an unattractive character. But in this particular episode she looks truly beautiful to me. Not just her appearance but her gentle 'damsel in distress' feminine personality. And her intelligence also shone through in this episode.

It was an incredible transformation. I remember thinking that her black hair looked so gorgeous and healthy. And thick and with nice curls. Beautiful like how Snow White's hair looks. And I have never generally regarded black hair to be nice. If I had, however, never seen her Klingon character and only saw her, I would probably think she looked more ordinary and not as attractive; but because I so often saw her ugly Klingon character with the facial deformations (in particular the ridges on the forehead), I thought the transformation in this episode was absolutely remarkable.

Women can be so attractive just by changing their appearance, and being more gentle.

CHAPTER

AGE 19

I REALLY FEEL THE LOVE TODAY. I think I know now. Yes. The specific formula. It was being tweaked for many months and years and I thought I had it right but NO, now I think I have it down to a science. I feel it right now. Yes I do. I really feel the love for decent females and the desire to be in a decent relationship. If I wanted to write a love poem now I know it would sound exceptional.

The only problem is that I don't have a target for my poem. Life feels so sweet right this minute. This love feeling is what I wanna feel forever. How about I just write a poem about this love feeling? A short and sweet one?

THE FEELING OF LOVE

What is this feeling, this feeling of love?
What brings us up like enchanted doves
Butterflies hovering in tendrils of air
And roses blooming in lovers lairs

What is this desire to hold someone near
What is this desire to caress her here
How can I express into words how I feel
Except that this feeling is wholly the real deal

Words cannot articulate how I feel / what I want
I want the world to experience,
this feeling and this font
To share and to bathe in the warmth of its glow
To rediscover what it is, will
rewrite all that we know

Pity the human who lives with no-feeling
Pity the fool who enjoys nothing but self-feeling
Today I wanna embrace in its magic
To not have it or not share it,
would be absolutely tragic

No more words, no more tones
No more expressions, no more zones
Only the enjoyment of a life fully lived
Only the appreciation of a life truly give'd.

CHAPTER

AGE 19

I **JUST DRANK A LARGE DOSE** of my love concoction again. And I just finished watching Star Trek Voyager S3 Ep 17. It's roughly about a female who lives her life backwards. But after watching it, I get the feeling that I am indeed moving back to a state of my life when I was younger. Was this puberty? Yes it was. The reason it feels this way is because the emotional state is so damn strong. It is like the body is full of teenage feelings and desires.

In any case, I really really like this feeling. I have a strong desire like I did as a young teenager, to hook up with a female and then have a relationship with her. Flirting with her. Being with her. Caring for her. Dancing with her. Spending time with her. Doing date stuff with her. Making each other happy. And yes. Making love with her (not just raw passion but love making).

Feels almost like getting crushes on beautiful girls of all nationalities; like when I was a young teenager. Still, this feeling is so damn great. It's like I am reliving or re-feeling how I felt in the past particularly during puberty. I feel it now. Even though there isn't really any main girl of interest, I'm just feeling the desire. I see how beautiful girls are. Their behaviors and styled hair styles and smiles and curves. They look so desirable. I freaking want to kiss their lips. I really do because I just know it will feel so damn good.

I would really like to be in a relationship with a pretty girl. I am finding many girls to be pretty at the moment. This feeling is so damn great! And based on the strength of the feelings right now, I will have to go to a party. No deal at all. I am only human. I am a bit scared of these feelings. They are so strong. Like when I was a young teenager. Yes. Going to a party soon. I freaking have to. The urge is strong like a teenager.

CHAPTER

AGE 20

VERY GOOD PROGRESS. I THINK I am getting there. I am hoping it anyway.

Strong physical functioning. Desire to make money. To work. To hook up. The ability and desire and confidence to flirt with and attract a female. A nice one that is. I'm feeling good about this love concoction. Extremely good. If I become energetically rich and powerful, and extremely attractive to females, I will know it is soon time to take on the world!

KEY TO YOUR HEART

Poems may not be the key to your heart
But poems are an expression,
a tribute and an art

A gratitude, to use to our devilish desires
To move the mind and soul, and alight spitfires

Having viewed many vids I
am emboldened to act
To express feelings and thoughts
in these comments of fact

You are beauty and genius deep to the core
Truly unique and magnificent,
something to adore

Your expression always genuine,
mostly lovely, and always true

This reaction was your best, truly
lovely and nothing less

A female of contrast you are, mostly
adorable, sometimes raw
It rubs the mind and heart until they are sore

If you enjoyed this poem then let me know
And more may come... just let it be so

CHAPTER

AGE 20

THIS AUDIO BOOK SERIES IS so corny. The audio series on this Anthony Ambrose guy (his name definitely sounds exotic). Like how he just inherited hundreds of millions of dollars worth of wealth from his family estate after they tested him for so many years, by making him live in poverty.

And all the actors fully exaggerate all the scenes and characters like how his ex girlfriend kept dissing him. No girl would do that man. She would just break up and that's it, not dis him repeatedly. But it is a story I have been interested in listening to. Cos it highlights a very interesting idea I have personally felt in the past.

Basically, the natural setting for males is that they should want to discretely show off their wealth and attractiveness to females. This is the easiest and fastest way to hook up and to mate and possibly find a suitable wife. Hiding your wealth, and family inheritance, or reputable job, or stuff like that won't achieve this. If you are super filthy rich or whatever then yeh, maybe hiding it a little bit is okay, but not to the extent of this Ambrose dude where he dresses poorly, for example.

Anyways, what I wanted to write about was that my ideas were all askew as a young teenager. During my international years, I was always into the allure of hiding my foreigner status and my attractiveness, by dressing normally and concealing my status and money from every girl. Yeh, it meant I didn't attract anywhere near as many females as I would have, if I hadn't tried so hard to hide my more attractive attributes. I always had in the back of my mind the thought that I was mysterious, and was a catch to the right girl who liked me for me and not my money, foreigner status, etc.

But I realize now that I was all mistaken.

Girls should be like I was. They should want a guy to like her for her appearance and her personality mainly. She doesn't want him to like her for her family or wealth or anything like that. And her appearance and personality is actually the most important things for a female to have. She must be like that because those attributes are critical for her role as a child bearer and mother. The other stuff shouldn't matter cos the girl wants the guy to stay with her through thick and thin even if she had nothing. The most important attributes of a female from the standpoint of finding a mate and reproducing is that she looks good and is the right body shape (childbearing body), and she is healthy and she is youthful and she has a nice, decent, caring and happy personality.

That is what matters.

For a guy, he must have money, wealth, status, accommodation, etc. All those things Western girls typically go for in a partner. Yeh, so the dude is not suppose to hide this stuff from a girl, especially one he is interested in.

I see all this now. I have seen it for the last few years but this audio series advertisement that I saw which lasted 20 minutes, has spurred on this idea again for me. Still, I will enjoy listening to some more of this sappy but interesting audio series.

P.S.

Why did I just load up the tinder app on my phone?

Why????????

CHAPTER

AGE 21

THIS FEELING IS NOT WRONG. At least I don't believe it is. This prowess is one piece of the proof of this. But alas, I'm not 100% sure yet. Being a man means being independent. Need to wait and see and let the results speak for itself. In my success and continued success and extraordinary success!

Feelings are quite important. Yes. You see a lion and you feel fear. You run or avoid it. You see a nice female and you feel a desire to talk to her. To flirt with her. You feel love perhaps? I have underestimated the power of feelings for a long time; maybe for most of my young life where I always thought they needed to be controlled. Feelings have a place in everyone's lives. They can push us. They can give us joy. They can make us better. They can get us into relationships, and get us to start families. They lead us to connect, or to be more social with others.

I really have underestimated feelings in my life up until this point. Yes, I have made some extraordinary revelations in my life. This I will put, quite high up on the list because it has taken me so long to truly appreciate it.

If you don't have the right feelings, then you are actually limited in a way. Not a life threatening limited of course, but you are not operating at peak performance levels.

I'm feeling it right now. I think I will drink my love concoction again soon. It is a masterpiece already, but it will become an immortal masterpiece.

CHAPTER

Eleven

AGE 21

BASICALLY, I HAVE BEGUN TO sense this new feeling I am experiencing. I have every now and then experienced it in the past, but I feel it fairly strongly right now. I feel like I need to work to make money. I feel like I want to get active, and do actions that will increase my net wealth.

I never felt this way when I was younger. It feels like a sense of urgency to make money. In fact, when I was younger, I remember thinking that earning money wasn't that important and shouldn't be something people should strive so hard to get. Work life balance was way more important, in my view.

But right now, I feel an urgency to work. I'm currently in an area of the city where people can play leisurely chess. And in fact I was planning on doing this. I wanted to play chess with the chess players here. But today, after taking my love concoction, I just feel like it might be a waste of time or that it is a waste of time. Despite sitting pretty on some valuable assets, and even though my business is doing OK (not great though), I feel like I need to make more money.

Why make more money? Why, for financial freedom, and to attract a female, and to settle down. Yes. I feel it. Business income is volatile. And I need to make alternative income streams. Playing leisurely chess is good if I already have a family and am extremely comfortable and secure financially; but not while I am still single, and not when my business situation is somewhat precarious.

Why do I feel this? I believe it is related to the emotional balance in the body. Yes. I believe this. So I should make money. Move into an apartment. Buy furniture. Buy things. Buy a nice car. And then get a female. Or the female first of course; or whenever possible.

That's what a male should strive for. A female on the other hand can be more focused on the home and household. Being idle for them is okay or even good, cos then they can become more specialized in bearing and raising children. They will be more receptive to male advances, and end up settling with those compatible, hard working, or financially successful males.

Far out. I really do believe.

No. This is not traditional thinking. This is evolution!

Twelve

AGE 21

I WANNA WRITE MORE ABOUT MY ideas on love and male and female mating relationships. Anyone who will likely be offended, do immediately turn away right this minute! It is very hard to believe that my love concoction has given me so many of these revelations, but it is all true!

Anyways, I was inspired to write here after hearing the lyrics of the song, "The way you make me feel" released in 1987, by Michael Jackson. In particular, the words that struck me were, "Oh, I'll be working from 9 to 5; to buy you things to keep you by my side." Maybe in our modern times, many females want to avoid being thought of as shallow gold diggers, and not want to openly look too interested when being the recipient of gifts from males, particularly valuable gifts; but there is no denying in my mind that the natural setting of human beings, particularly for females, is that they want to receive gifts from their male partner (including jewels and other valuable items), and the male partner naturally wants to give it to the female.

I truly believe this now.

Females (who are natural and healthy and fertile) are naturally more inclined towards the family, and not wanting to work and are highly receptive to potential male dates who are generous to them, and who give them valuable gifts. The females are more carefree in my opinion, in terms of not wanting to work in employment, and they want males to do all the income producing work and money making in the relationship. They would be more than happy in their element of maintaining the household and keeping up appearances, and supporting their husbands in a supportive role in the home, and by offering emotional support, and raising their kids. But they want/need the male partner to bring home the bacon and to be well liked in society.

I have been trying to tweak the love concoction so that it makes me consistently want to work hard and bring in the bacon. Because I believe this to be the natural setting of most human males. When you have the bacon, then the female will be naturally so so attracted to you, that almost nothing you do will be perceived as a turn off. The wiring and sparks in the natural female minds, will not allow them to dislike you when you are a good, natural, hardworking, and masculine provider of the relationship.

Lazy males in the past rarely got married or had kids (unless they were rich from relatives or similar reasons).

CHAPTER

Thirteen

AGE 22

THE CURRENT VERSION OF MY love concoction is truly extraordinary. It is so powerful in turning humans into the most enchanting versions of themselves. I really feel this power with the females. It just feels so much more natural and easy and fun. It is fun to flirt, and I frequently and consistently get a positive reaction from them now.

It feels natural. It feels natural.

Plus I take actions that help with the process. My mind just naturally tells me the things I should do. For example, I make a lot of jokes with the girls and they dig it all up. They really do. They just feel really happy and laugh out loud and laugh laugh laugh. It has usually worked well with receptionists and waitresses in the past, but now it is frequently working with ALL the decent females.

Really amazing. What else? If I find out a chick has a boyfriend, 90% of the time now I will discontinue the relationship with them or pursuit of them. Why? It just seems so obvious now. Because it is a waste of time. The girl is practically engaged and there will always be that obstacle to me dating her. And it would be slack on her actual boyfriend. And because I'll be a home wrecker. It seems so freaking obvious now.

I'm not totally ruling it out though. If the girl shows interest then I could continue cos it then likely means she is unhappy with her current relationship, and hanging out with her would be a lot easier. But otherwise, it would be too much work and too difficult to pursue the relationship. But once again, jokes are a big thing. They just end up laughing a lot.

If I am short of time like I was once today with the tram chick, who was going to get off the tram after a few stops, then I tell her my job or business and ask her if she was interested in that. If she was, then she would have much more easily given me her number or facebook. Otherwise there wouldn't have been enough time to get her details. I basically go straight to the most important thing a girl looks for in a guy. She wants to know what his job is or what he does for a living.

What else do I do differently which I didn't really do before now? I'm more casual overall. Not messaging the girl too much or sending her overly long messages. I don't bring up any question of asking her out too early. There's no need for that. The communication and flirting with her is fun already. And that is the getting to know her part. The dates can come later if they come at all. I take it one slow step at a time. The most important thing is to be casual about it.

I suppose I kind of flirt a bit more when I am on my love concoction. Maybe. Not sure. I just say what comes natural. Not trying to be smooth or anything. I don't come on too strong too soon anymore. Like no overly sensitive and powerful poems. I'm not ruling out sending a girl poems, but not until I really start to like her and only after a while. When I have just met her, why should I send her a poem so soon? It means I am coming on too strong doesn't it?

What else?

I casually say stuff that females hold in high regard. Like I tell them I am living in Amberville. Amberville is an expensive and posh area. It makes me look solid (and successful). It hits the exact right chords in a female's psyche. I make it sound like I am successful.

I am surprised. I feel almost like a different person with the level of success I have been getting. I have unlocked a part of me all humans should have.

CHAPTER

Fourteen

AGE 22

I WATCHED SOME OF THE MOVIE, "The Thirteenth Floor" again yesterday.

The one thing I thought as I was watching that movie was that the female character was so hot. When she wore those nice clothes and went into the character as the developer's daughter (as opposed to the checkout chick) she was so hot. I had thought this in the past upon watching the movie, but last night I really thought it.

She was such a beautiful, decent, gorgeous and desirable female. So gorgeous. Gorgeous feminine gentle personality as well. And she was a movie star. She ended up marrying a writer (I will become the best writer on the planet - so she was just my type!).

Her hair had beautiful curls. And it was a beautiful color. Her figure was really nice as well. She was marriage material for sure.

AT FIRST SIGHT

At first sight there was no feeling
At first sight the barrier withheld
Professional etiquette blurred out the attraction
Causing inaction to reign supreme
I caught but a glimpse yet your
attraction has hit me
And now pulsing through my blood is
the intoxicant of your loveliness

CHAPTER

AGE 23

EVERYTHING I THINK I KNOW about love and male and female relationships I will wipe clear as of today. It is this feeling, and these feelings towards this female, that tells me all I need to know. It is as strong as an instinct. I haven't felt as strongly like this since I was a young teenager. I remember really desiring certain females back then. And it wasn't a crazy sexual lust. No. It was more of a desire to be in a relationship, or to merely spend time with that person.

Yes. Means is important. But equally important is this genuine desire to be in a relationship and to get to know the female. After all, presumably, she could end up being the mother of your kids. So where is the love and genuine desire to be in a relationship?

This feeling is truly powerful. It is this feeling of susceptibility and desire. It is this growing attraction, care, and dare I say even love for another person. To like a girl more and more as you get to know her, in a way where her personality makes her look more beautiful than when you first saw her. When you first saw her, she looked good to you but not beautiful. But now she is becoming the only one you have your attention on.

You feel like you are not good enough for her, but you still want to go for it. To chase her? And because she seemed to show a genuine interest back, I am falling. Her smiles from my jokes is all I seem to respond to. It is like, you are prepared to redirect your entire life to give that relationship a chance. Because the relationship is more important than mere survival, so you strive to achieve success a different way.

Should a guy give a girl he likes money? My feeling is yes, but it needs to be done in a discrete way that doesn't seem to her like he is trying to buy her love. He can give her anything else as well including gifts and jewels and whatever, but only if it seems like she wants to receive it from him.

Why is this? It is because if a man likes a girl (in the way nature intended), then this means he cares for her (and not just wants to lie with her and leave). If he cares for her and genuinely cares for her, wouldn't it make sense that he will wanna give her things to increase her comfort and living standard or simply to make her happy? Why would his act of giving then, be perceived as wrong to the girl? The answer is it won't so long as the girl likes him enough to want to accept the gift and continue the relationship. And so long as the dude is not so rough about it or gives it in a way that doesn't show her he likes her (or maybe respects her).

The movie "Blue Crush" had a good scene where the male star hired the female to give him surfing lessons. Yes the dude was smooth (and rich) and really wanted to use that surfing lesson as an excuse to date her. And he paid her extremely well in advance for the lessons, in that scene in the hotel room. He had the means to. And he wasn't tight. And she loved him for it. It helped that she was financially cash strapped though.

CHAPTER

Sixteen

AGE 23

J WANT TO ELABORATE A BIT more on my current thoughts about gift giving and money giving to a female you like. Basically, when you give to the girl, you must be discrete about it and if anything, make it look like you are doing it because you care for her and want her to be happy, and not because you want to buy her love or to just get physical with her.

The way this is done is to be discrete about it and not make it too obvious. You can't make her feel embarrassed that she has accepted the gift or money from you when deep down she wants to accept it. It can't seem like you care so much about the gift that you will be a loser and demand it back if she doesn't respond to you in return. If you are discrete, then this also shows you care about her dignity, and her opinion, etc. The gift giving must be so matter of fact that it doesn't even register in her mind that you have given her a gift.

Man. It is like pigeons flying around and looking for nests to lay their eggs. They are looking at real estate and the partner or the bird that made the nest to attract her in the first place is a secondary afterthought. The female bird will let the male bird mate with her if she likes his nest. It doesn't even cross the female bird's mind that she has trespassed on his property, or in the least will be living there with him.

It is just such a matter or fact, standard instinctive response or expectation by the female bird, that the male bird must have a nice nest.

In regards to human females, this is the same in the matter of gift giving and perhaps also of marriage. It is just expected instinctively by the girl that a guy who loves her will marry her, so that their relationship becomes recognized by society and she is protected in the event of his accidental death. She and his kids (and her kids) will still have some security or safety net or nest egg.

So the gift giving is so matter of fact and expected by her, that if you give to her and make it look like it is not a standard courting action of a male, and that you expect something from her in return, she will be absolutely disgusted by your actions. It is exactly like how a male is expected to pay for the date for the girl. Definitely at least for the first few dates while they are still on the courtship or getting to know each other stage.

I suppose the gift giving is also a measure of a man's means but not necessarily. Also, a guy could be filthy rich but if he isn't willing to share any of the wealth with her, then from her perspective he is exactly like a normal wealth or poor wealth person. From her perspective, it is how willing the guy is to give to the relationship that counts more than his actual capability to give in the relationship. So the gift giving symbolizes both the guy's means and the guy's willingness to give. It is by no means a perfect system, but it is the system that has been honed through evolution.

The part about showing the girl the guy's means can happen in a different way, such as by showing her his job and income, or his house, or cars, or special passport or whatever. These things, the guy should actually want to let the girl know cos these things should be recognized by the guy as things girls value from a partner. In this matter as well, he should be discrete and not be show-offy about it.

Like if he owns a nice car then show it to her discretely (like those YouTube gold digger video pranks where the dude purposely tries to pick up the girl in a lame-ass way, and is otherwise then rejected, and then he drives away in his Lamborghini). If he has a great job then he can tell her but not be too show-offy about it. If he has a nice house then he can show her photos of himself in front of it with his family, so it looks like he is just trying to show her pictures of his family. He can just say, these are photos of his parents with his house behind; "Here's a photo of me and my parents."… She asks, "Whose house is that?" He answers, "Oh, it's my house, I bought it a few years ago."

All in all, the act of giving gifts or money really all comes back to the dude's willingness to share this wealth with her, which is arguably more important than simply how much wealth the dude has. How can anyone argue with my analysis?

CHAPTER

Seventeen

AGE 24

THE FEMALE HAS ASKED ME via text message if I have 'habere prosperitas' yet. I am guessing it is a religious activity or sounds like a religious activity. I don't think it is a Christian activity and is most likely a Buddhist activity like visiting the temple or Buddhist statue. I've messaged her and asked her what it means.

Religion. A mismatch here can definitely kill the relationship. It is unavoidable. I consider myself an atheist although I was raised a Christian by my family (that is to say, I went to Church when I was younger and got baptized and all that). I became atheist probably around age 16 - 17. I remember questioning my beliefs around this time. Of course, I still did all the Christian things expected of me for a while longer. I can't quite remember when I stopped going to church weekly.

There was another chick I used to know who I went out briefly with, when I was about 18 years of age I think it was. She was from my old high school and was quite a devout Christian. The relationship and even friendship died as soon as she learned I wasn't a believer.

I still remember her expression in the car when I told her something like it. She was very sad and shocked and said something like, "Why did you say that!" Or maybe it was, "Why did you do that!"

And the rest of the ride home was brief. And then I never heard from her again.

OK. An internet search tells me 'habere prosperitas' means to acquire prosperity. How am I to answer her? She is definitely the type of girl who likes money in a partner. How am I to answer her? If the male bird does not have a nice nest, the female bird will not park herself there.

CHAPTER

Eighteen

AGE 24

FOR AMELIA

The sun rises and the moon sets
A whole new day starts anew
I think of you in all your beauty
And suddenly the sky reflects more blue!

Our time together has been short
Our time together has been new
But in these few times of June
The like is real, the like is true @};---'

I do not know if you like poems
And I do not know if you will spew
But with this poem I give a memory
A stamp, a record, for me and you ;-D

You are only Amelia Stromer
And I am only Tristan DeBoo
But our worlds came together
when no others did
And because of this I thank you (⌐■_■)

Nineteen

AGE 24

I JUST DRANK YET AGAIN MY love concoction.

I feel more sympathetic and empathetic towards other humans now, but also more desiring or wanting of those things humans (males in particular) should all strive for, namely getting into a relationship and starting a family and being financially settled. I really feel like I wanna be a good male for a female person. I feel like I need to get to work and make money.

Coitus is no longer just about copulation and reproduction, but also about love making now. And I really notice the background and suitability of females I am attracted to. I feel like I wanna impress the female's parents so they accept me and I am welcomed into the family. It is all a true desire to be with the female. The right female. It isn't about reproducing for numbers. Man, as a real man, you have to be there for the female and support her and make her happy. I really actually wanna spend time with her, and all her feminine characteristics really makes me like her all the more.

This means that to her, masculine characteristics must make her like me more as well. What are these characteristics? Wealth. Humor. Looking after yourself. Living independently. Chivalry. Being proactive. Chasing her to show you really like her genuinely, as she really responds to a guy who genuinely likes/loves her and cares for her.

A few females in my past life I have felt the same way as now, but I never pursued them due to lack of the right circumstances. One was someone who now lives in Europe with her fiance. Another was a staff member at a previous place I had worked with. Both very decent females. It is the word decent that seems to stand out. Not indecent. Not socially unliked females. But decent females with decent families.

OK. I am a very strong believer that emotions are there to get humans to behave the way humans are suppose to behave, and to therefore assist in their mating/survival actions. Here's a poem I just wrote to prove it.

POETIC PROOF OF LIFE
CHANGED FOREVER

Laying on my bed, the colors all look
vivid, as my beating heart pumps
charged blood through my system.

I reflect on the moment, I reflect on
the feeling, nothing is more cherished
than this moment of precision.

Like a teen in his youth, the years from then to
now fade away, way away, into the moment.

The realization of what life can be, what life will
be, and what life has become, roars like a sonant.

What is it people say? That poems show love?

The language communicates gracefully
like a dove. Fitting like a glove into a world
from above. Where meaning blurs into
obscurity... and meaning fades of purity.

Alas, it is irrelevant! Cos I say, today;
something has come alive. A dormant
beast, bearing the power of a million suns,
and the wonder of a million rainbows.

The charm, the surreality, of love, of
life, of dreams, and of wonder... in
a world filled with meadows.

CHAPTER

AGE 24

Just watch these movies from America before the 1960's. The girls then were so decent and less lustful. Female chastity actually existed before marriage. Watch some of those scenes like the one in the movie "Happy Go Lovely (1951)". During scenes where the guy accidentally entered the women's changing room, all the women got all fully embarrassed and the dude instinctively covered his eyes with the item.

That stuff would never happen anywhere in the world nowadays. But the typical family where there is a husband breadwinner and a wife child rearer is actually the way it was, and was assumed to be, all throughout human history up until recent times. Women were assumed to want to stay in the home and to hook up with that one person who could provide for her and who loved her. And the average man was supposed to wanna marry that right, conservative, homely (and preferably even celibate) female to start a family with.

This is traditional thinking, but there is a reason it is called traditional. It is because this is the standard or normal thinking method of humans all throughout human history. Women in the 1950's and before then actually wanted to save themselves for marriage. It was something that was common and respected and even expected. I see all these things now because of my... love concoction.

Look at the movies from the 1920's and 30's, right through to the 1990's and 2000's. The more recent the year of the movie, the more free and open the females and males were. The older the year of the movie, the more conservative and traditional the females and males were. I have to be onto something.

CHAPTER

Twenty-One

THE FINAL CHAPTER

AGE 24

NOW FINALLY, BACK TO THE situation with my new love interest. I really do like her. She is marriage material for sure. Based on all the conversations and experiences I've had with her to date, this is how I feel. She seems popular with her co-workers and friends. And she's a hard worker with a kind heart. Plus she's more feminine I reckon than most females.

And living and settling down in a good city has always been one of my biggest goals/plans. Despite the huge amounts of traveling I have done in my life; settling down in one place has always been in the cards for me. And I feel like this girl is such high quality. She is just so sweet. I am conflicted though because this country she lives in, is not the country I see myself living in. But no.

Enough of all this deliberation. It's time for me to take the next steps. I'm going to stop with all these entries and just get on with it, and do what has to be done. This is the end of this story. This is the end of this journey. I will start a new journey now; a journey which is yet to be written, and a journey which I may write about again in my next writings.

END OF BOOK